Animals in My World

AWESOME ANIMAL TAILS

Edison Booth

HABA®

PowerKiDS press.

NEW YORK

Published in 2018 by The Rosen Publishing Group, Inc.
29 East 21st Street, New York, NY 10010

First Edition

Editor: Melissa Raé Shofner
Book Design: Michael Flynn

Photo Credits: Cover Joshua Francis/Shutterstock.com; p. 5 Flip de Nooyer/Minden Pictures/Getty Images; pp. 6, 24 (bill) Tadas_Jucys/Shutterstock.com; pp. 9, 24 (feathers) duangnapa_b/Shutterstock.com; p. 10 Tawin Mukdharakosa/Shutterstock.com; pp. 13, 24 (tail) Gil.K/Shutterstock.com; p. 14 Paisan Changhirun/Shutterstock.com; p. 17 Raoul Eric/EyeEm Premium/Getty Images; p. 18 Kathy Kay/Shutterstock.com; p. 21 jeep2499/Shutterstock.com; p. 22 (inset) Savo Ilic/Shutterstock.com; p. 22 Peter Reijners/Shutterstock.com.

Cataloging-in-Publication Data

Names: Booth, Edison.
Title: Awesome animal tails / Edison Booth.
Description: New York : PowerKids Press, 2018. | Series: Animals in my world | Includes index.
Identifiers: ISBN 9781538321447 (pbk.) | ISBN 9781538321461 (library bound) | ISBN 9781538321454 (6 pack)
Subjects: LCSH: Body covering (Anatomy)–Juvenile literature. | Wings (Anatomy)–Juvenile literature. | Tail–Juvenile literature. | Fur–Juvenile literature.
Classification: LCC QL941.B644 2018 | DDC 591.47–dc23

Manufactured in the United States of America

CPSIA Compliance Information: Batch #BS17PK: For Further Information contact Rosen Publishing, New York, New York at 1-800-237-9932

Please visit: www.rosenpublishing.com and www.habausa.com

CONTENTS

Terrific Tails

All sorts of animals live in the jungle. Some have tails that help them swim or climb. What do animals of the jungle look like?

Jungle Birds

Toucans are birds. They have long tail feathers. Their feathers are black. Toucans have a big, bright bill. Their bill helps them grab food. Toucans also have blue feet.

Parrots are birds. They have long tail feathers. Parrots can be many bright colors. They have big wings. There are lines around their eyes.

Long Tails

Crocodiles have a long tail. Their tail helps them swim. Crocodiles have sharp teeth and short legs. Crocodiles can weigh a lot. Their eyes are small and black.

Lemurs have soft, gray fur. They have yellow eyes. Lemurs have a long tail. Their tail has black-and-white stripes. Lemurs use their tail to balance in the trees.

Tigers are big cats. They have orange fur with black stripes. Tigers have four paws. They have sharp teeth and claws. Tigers use their long tail for balance.

Jaguars are big cats. They have sharp teeth and claws. Jaguars use their long tail for balance. They have orange fur and lots of black spots.

Chameleons have skin that can change colors. Chameleons have a long tail. They use their tail to grab branches. Chameleons can move their eyes in different directions.

No Tails?

Orangutans are apes. Apes don't have tails. Orangutans have orange fur. They have two long arms. They use their hands and feet to climb. Orangutans love to be in trees.

tadpoles

Tree frogs live in trees. They have a tail when they are tadpoles. Tadpoles use their tail to swim. Adult tree frogs don't have a tail. They have sticky feet so they can climb.

WORDS TO KNOW

bill

feathers

tail

INDEX